The Little Iceberg

First published in Great Britain in 2020

Copyright © 2020 connected baby Ltd

 connected baby

All rights reserved

ISBN 978-1-963040-0-0

Text © 2019 Nicky Murray
Illustrations © 2019 Sylvia Lynch

Font: Maqueen Sans
Paper: Revive Recycled Matt Silk 200gsm

The *connected baby* team:
    Design: Brett Housego
    Trauma specialist: Dr Suzanne Zeedyk
    Nature specialist: Pete Kinnear

Printed and bound: H B Rutherford, Broughty Ferry

The Little Iceberg

Written by Nicky Murray

Illustrated by Sylvia Lynch

The water stretched for as far as the eye could see. You would be forgiven for thinking someone had drawn a thick blue line and coloured in the bottom half of the drawing, completely. Well, almost completely.

In this grand and majestic ocean, there floated a speck, a jagged piece of...something...I don't know what. But it was, it most definitely was!

When you looked closer, that speck was an iceberg. Floating.
Alone. Far from anywhere.

She had once belonged to an ice shelf. But that was before she
calved off and had become lost to the push and pull of the icy swells.

Now she was drifting, on her own, getting colder and colder,
harder and harder. No one pays much attention. After all,
there are lots of icebergs in the ocean, all shapes and sizes.

The little iceberg grew sad. Everyone seemed scared of her,
even though, deep down, it was the last thing she wanted.

I'll let you into a secret. She was frightened all the time herself.

Anytime anyone came close, they would crash against her and end up hurting themselves. She had been the cause of many tears and raised voices. All because strangers had come too close.

So she grew harder, as it got colder. She became so hard, with so much hidden beneath the surface, no one could get anywhere near her.

One day a little bird appeared. She slipped slightly as she landed.
But then the little bird said nothing and pretty much did nothing,
as far as the iceberg could tell. For the whole of the day! Nothing!

She didn't move much. She was just happy to be there, on the cool,
thick, blue ice.

When it started to get dark, the little bird flew off without a sound.
The iceberg noticed she had left a tiny twig, right there on the ice shelf.

"I wonder what that little bird is up to?" thought the iceberg.
"I wonder if she'll come back?"

"Actually, I don't care if she does come back, silly little bird."
The iceberg closed her eyes as all around the whales sang
their haunting songs.

The very next day the bird returned. She hovered gently above the iceberg, as if waiting on an invitation to land.

When she did, it was so lightly the iceberg didn't even feel her touch. This time it was in a different place from the last, don't you know? How strange.

The little bird seemed to be watching, her head tilted to the side, as if she were listening to the shifting of the ice. It creaked and groaned like an old pirate's knees, the bones made weak by years of scrubbing the decks and being soaked by the salty sea.

The little bird looked slowly and very, very carefully at the ice...
the white crystals, the scars, the twists, the scratches, the watery blue
diamonds, the buffs, the scuffs and seams.

She looked so intently, I swear it was as if she was trying to see
through the ice itself. But that was impossible...especially on the
upper ridges, which were thick and crusted like angry waves that
had frozen in time.

Up and down, from side to side and back again. Then whoosh!
off she flew, just as the dark started to set in. Again the iceberg
noticed a tiny twig and the scent that came from it.

"What a strange bird who would bring such things to me!"
thought the iceberg. She closed her eyes tight, as a shark
bumped into her and thrashed its tail in fright.

On the third day, without so much as a word, the bird began pecking away at the hard bits on the upper ridges. That's where I was talking about before... the part that looked like the lip of a glassy wave just before it breaks at its highest point, before spraying the world with its white water.

All day, every day...

...little touches of her beak. Then at long last, a piece of ice was freed and fell into the sea. The iceberg felt much better, a bit like when you are carrying something heavy, far too heavy, and you get a chance to put it down. Or better still, like when someone asks if they can help by carrying it for a while.

Every morning the little bird would arrive and pause for
a moment. She would listen to the creaks and groans of
the iceberg.

"This must be a very clever bird," thought the iceberg.
"How do you know where to start each day, little bird?"
The bird cocked her tiny head to one side and replied,
"I listen."

One day a big piece of ice fell off and nearly crushed the little bird. She flew away and didn't come back all the rest of that day.

The iceberg was very sad.

"Where did you go?" she asked the next day.
"I went to find my friend," said the little bird without lifting her head. "What's your friend called?"
"Courage," replied the little bird, and kept pecking.

The iceberg didn't like the fact the little bird had left her suddenly, so she growled at the bird all day. The growling got louder and louder until suddenly the little bird began to sing.

She sang the same song over and over and over. "What's the name of that song?" snapped the iceberg. "It's called Compassion," answered the bird.

Very soon the little iceberg stopped groaning. She started listening to the beautiful singing, which echoed far across the ocean. At times, the little iceberg hummed along too.

Some days the little bird would work all through the evening, long into the night. This happened especially when she was trying to open up a large crack in the ice and wouldn't stop 'til the work was done.

"What a determined little bird. She must be so tired, working without rest," thought the iceberg. "I will help her." She began to move and sway with the bird. Suddenly the crack became wider and the ice came tumbling down, as easily as a knife slicing through warm butter.

Except it wasn't butter, was it? It was thick, twisted ice, and the white, jagged pillars were falling away into the green water, tumbling, somersaulting, splashing into the deep waters below.

Day after day after day, the little bird worked. She would often slip and fall, but she would not make a fuss. Sometimes she would shiver, but she wouldn't give up. No matter how cold or fierce the wind blew, the little bird always stayed connected.

One day a terrible storm came from nowhere, as if it had been hiding in the thick clouds high up in the sky. By now, the two of them were used to storms that came often and without warning. But this storm, that night, was like no other.

The clouds were dark, as if someone had taken a brush full of black paint and plunged it into a jam jar full of clear water, and then started to stir, Fast, Faster, Furious.

The iceberg was frightened. She shook as electric bolts clattered all around. The little bird said, "You are safe. I am here. This will pass."

She waited. "What do you need from me?"
"Hold on tight!" cried the iceberg, and the little bird did just as she asked.

Small cracks formed beneath her grip and spread quickly, weaving themselves together. They opened a cave deep inside the iceberg. It echoed with their singing, like a gentle murmuring heartbeat.

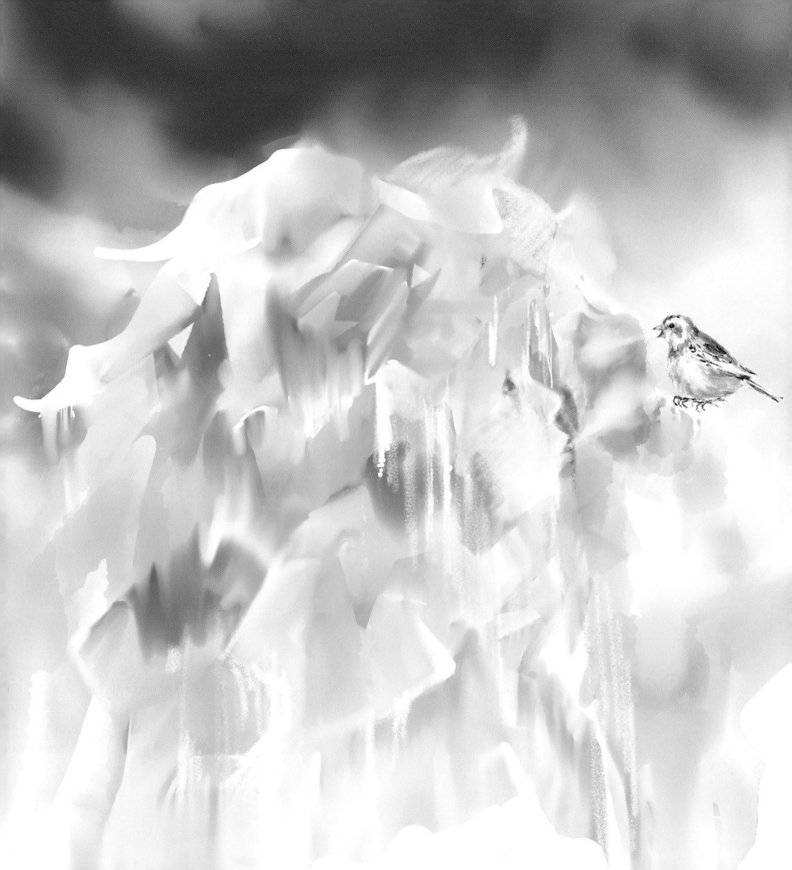

So the storm passed, and both the iceberg and the bird breathed in the fresh air. It was as if they were freed, having been submerged beneath the waves for so very long.

They had fun breathing to counts of four, then five, then six, and starting all over again. "What a marvellous thing breath is!" said the iceberg as she watched the bird's belly rise and fall. White smoke came out of her beak.

The iceberg thought, "What a powerful thing imagination is, if it can make a fire-breathing dragon out of a tiny bird's breath."

One day the little iceberg realised she had very little ice left. As soon as she thought that, the little bird said, "And so, our work is done. I must go." And she spread her wings and rose into the air.

"But wait, what is your name, little bird?" asked the tiny piece of ice. In all the time they had been together, she had never thought to ask. Being together, connected, had somehow been enough.

The bird swooped low, and sang out one word,
"Kindness." She hovered for an instant, giving the
little iceberg a tiny kiss, and then she was gone.

The little iceberg was melting and afraid she might disappear into the deep. She was used to the chill that loneliness brings. But then she remembered how brave her Friend had been, so she trusted with all her heart, closed her eyes and...

...when she opened them, she was part of the ocean!

Cool and clear, she could see the colours of the rainbow in the fish and the plants beneath the surface. She felt part of the world for the very first time.

Now and then she would look up and see tiny birds flying overhead and smile, because she knew the secret to happiness was kindness.

A brave little bird who listened and stayed connected, no matter how fiercely the wind blew, singing songs of compassion, had taught her that.